RC
& Little Putt-Putt
GO DOWN SWINGING

Timothy Friend

ROCKET RYDER
& Little Putt-Putt
GO DOWN SWINGING

Timothy Friend

Coffin Hop Press

CALGARY, ALBERTA, CANADA

Rocket Ryder & Little Putt-Putt Go Down Swinging

Copyright © 2018 Coffin Hop Press Ltd

All rights reserved. No part of this publication may be reproduced, distributed or transmitted in any form or by any means, including photocopying, recording, or other electronic or mechanical methods, without the prior written permission of the publisher, except in the case of brief quotations embodied in critical reviews and certain other noncommercial uses permitted by copyright law. For permission requests, write to the publisher, addressed "Attention: Permissions Coordinator," at the address below.

Coffin Hop Press Ltd
200 Rivervalley Crescent SE
Calgary, Alberta CANADA T2C 3K8
www.coffinhop.com
mailto:**info@coffinhop.com**

Cover Design ©2018 Coffin Hop Press Ltd
Cover elements:Shutterstock ID: 55854769 jmcdermottillo;
Shutterstock ID: 73664011 MilousSK
Book Layout ©2018 Coffin Hop Press

Ordering Information:
Quantity sales. Special discounts may be available on quantity purchases by corporations, associations, and others. For details, contact the "Special Sales Department" at the address above.

Rocket Ryder & Little Putt-Putt Go Down Swinging/ Timothy Friend —1st ed. Paperback

ISBN 978-1-988987-00-2

*For Jenn,
the star of my favorite show.
25 seasons and counting.*

*"Play with murder enough and it gets to you
one of two ways.
It makes you sick, or you get to like it."*

— Dashiell Hammett, *Red Harvest*

1

Rocket Ryder, our brave captain and a decorated officer in the United Worlds Space Patrol, was too damn drunk to fire the reverse thrusters. Even as our badly damaged star-cruiser drifted toward certain destruction all he could do was slap his hand around on the plywood console, taking a few missed jabs at the red-painted cardboard button. He finally gave up, rested his face in his hands. Our foley guy hit the cue anyway and the roar of rocket engines filled the soundstage.

This was in August 1953.

We all knew Rick was a heavy drinker, but he'd never let his off-screen shenanigans affect his work. Lately though he had trouble remembering his lines. He'd taken to writing them on index cards and hiding them around the set. Sometimes his speech was slurred. I wasn't sure how much longer Lyle was going to put up with him. Even the producer of a bottom-of-the-barrel kiddie show like ours had standards.

As the sound of the thrusters faded, Rick said, in the hammy stentorian tone he used for Ryder, "It's no use. We don't have enough power to resist the frozen star's gravitational pulse."

Pulse? Jesus Christ.

"Oh, no," I said from where I floated on Soundstage 2. "There must be some way to escape its pull." I over-enunciated the word 'pull', the closest I could come to correcting him on live television.

I couldn't see Rick's face, but I could plainly hear the irritation in his voice when he said, "I'm sorry, Putt-Putt, but there is no escape. A frozen star is so dark, and its pull so strong that even light cannot escape. This is it, my friend. Our final journey. Today we travel into an eternal stygian darkness unlike anything we've ever known."

The harness I wore was smashing my balls. I gritted my teeth, trying not to let the pain show, as I looked directly into the camera, just like always, and said, just like always, "Suffering Satellites! Can this really be the end?"

The speakers high up on the wall near the viewing window blasted out our theme song as Deke brought the library cue up and over. I could see Ernie in the production booth, hands waving like a conductor as he gave instructions to the various folks around him.

There was no sign of Lyle, but it was rare that our producer made an appearance at the studio. His father, Dominic Vincitore, owned the station and had given Lyle the job of producer in the hope that having some responsibility would leave him less time for carousing and gambling. So far no go. Lyle Vincitore was not the type to allow anything as trivial as a job get in the way of his good time.

Dominic couldn't have been all that surprised. He'd been a hell-raiser himself in his younger days, before mostly retiring from extortion and arson to focus his energies on politics. These days, as a grey haired alderman,

Dom was almost never seen in the company of underworld types, and he aspired to respectability. KCTO was his shot at running a legitimate business.

Having delivered my final line, I remained frozen in place, staring awkwardly into the camera until I heard Ernie say from up in the booth, "And we're out. That's a wrap for the week. Good work guys."

Good work? I'd expected him to lay into Rick for his drunken performance. Or at least chew me out for correcting him. Ernie's temper usually ran at a low boil and it didn't take much to make him steam. Empty compliments were not his style.

Soundstage 2 was nothing more than the back corner of Soundstage 1 blocked off by a heavy black curtain. I heard the announcer begin hawking breakfast cereal and a second later Rick yanked the curtain aside and stormed over to where I hung from wires in front of a starry backdrop. On the ground I was six inches shorter than him, but in harness we were able to argue face to face; Rick's pale and sweaty, mine pinched and twisted from the agony of my crushed nuts.

"I swear to God, Scotty," Rick said. "You ever give me a line reading again and I'll bounce your head off the wall."

"Then learn your damn lines," I said. "If that's too much for you then at least learn to read, you fucking lush."

If the kids could see us like this. Rick Tanner and Scotty Crane were known to children all over Kansas City, at least those who had decent reception and bothered to tune in to KCTO at 3:00 p.m. on weekdays, as Rocket Ryder and Little Putt-Putt. Our characters were pals, loyal and brave, even though the actors who played them could barely stand one another.

I can't say that Rick had anything personal against me since he was an asshole to everyone, but for my part, I hated the man the moment I first laid eyes on him. I told myself I hated his cocky attitude, his lackadaisical work ethic, his bad acting and his drunken behavior. More than any of that, though, I hated his good looks. His chiseled features, thick black hair, bright blue eyes, all made me want to break a bottle over his head. He was catnip to girls, women and grandmothers alike. Being around him all the time made me painfully aware of my own shortcomings.

We tried to keep our dislike of one another under wraps, and so far we'd succeeded. The Adventures of Rocket Ryder in Space had been on the air for two years now and we had a small following among the kindergarten set. We weren't inspiring any fan clubs, but our characters were popular enough that Rick and I were occasionally asked to appear at a few public events. Rocket and Putt-Putt had been guests at the grand openings of two grocery stores and a barber shop. We'd even hosted an elementary school party at a local roller-rink. Unfortunately that last one ended with Rick guzzling two bottles of cheap tequila and vomiting in front of the PTA, which put the kibosh on any future public appearances. Such is the life of a celebrity.

"I'm warning you, gimp," Rick said. "Don't fuck with me."

"Kiss my flying ass," I said. "Learn. Your. Lines."

"It doesn't matter," Rick said, "Even if the knuckleheads could understand the gibberish, it just doesn't matter."

Before I could ask him what he was talking about, Rick gave my shoulder a hard shove that set me to spinning, then brushed through the curtain and was gone. I yelled a few foul words at him but got no response, and started to feel queasy when the rig twisted up and began its backspin. Just then someone grabbed me by the collar and jerked me to an abrupt halt and I found myself staring at the gloomy mug of our director, Ernie Vincent.

Ernie said, "Well, look who's here. If I knew you were coming, I'd've baked a cake."

I forced a smile, but didn't say anything.

Ernie dragged a step-ladder over and guided me onto it, letting me lean on him until I could get my weight shifted to my good leg. I slipped out of the rig, climbed down from the ladder, and limped across the soundstage to the Captain's seat.

The seat was really just a sprung office chair painted silver, a pair of wobbly antennae glued to the arm rests. I sat down carefully. Partly out of concern for my tender balls, but mostly because the chair was unstable. It had toppled over once while we were on the air, sending Rick sprawling. He'd never been a good actor, but he had been sharper then and managed to hastily improvise a bit about space-turbulence that was so funny I'd bitten my cheek bloody trying not to bust up on camera.

"I think that was the roughest one yet," I said. "If he fucks up like that again I'm going to flatten him."

Ernie said, "And be the first person to buy the farm on live television."

I rubbed at my chest, thinking of little Yobo nestled in close to my heart. I stopped as soon as I realized what I was doing.

"Worth it," I said. "Plus it would be good for the ratings."

Ernie all at once found the tops of his shoes very interesting.

"What's up?" I asked.

Ernie shook his head.

"You're shit at keeping secrets," I said. "Give."

"I'm not supposed to tell anyone this, but. . ." Ernie gave a little shrug, then said, "We're done."

"Done? You mean done, done? Cancelled?"

Ernie nodded, said, "Yup. Station's been bought. As of Monday we'll be owned by DuMont."

"A network? But we're UHF. What's the point?"

"All I know is DuMont didn't get the licenses they wanted," Ernie said, "and they're desperate. The details are above my pay grade, but Old Man Vincitore signed the papers last night and I've heard we're not the only ones getting the ax."

"Just the first," I said. "You tell Rick yet?"

Ernie let out a breath, "Yeah, told him earlier. Thinking now I should've waited till after the show."

I sat silently for a moment, trying come to grips with my sudden lack of employment. "So what the hell are they going to run in our slot?"

2

"Buck Rogers," I said. "That's what they plan to replace us with. Probably Lyle's idea."

Sally set a cup of coffee in front of me and took her place across from me at our small kitchen table. She said, "Lyle? Isn't he out too?"

"Of course not," I said. "Apparently that was part of the deal. Lyle is the new station manager. We all lose our jobs, meanwhile the boss's useless son gets a promotion. Those fat-cats always look out for their own. You can count on that sure as the rising of the sun."

Sally reached over and rested her hand on mine, "Take it easy. You don't want to get yourself worked up."

I took a breath, nodded.

Sally said, "Are they going to find something else for you?"

"Not likely. I'm only working now because Ernie got me the job. He's out too, and with my condition. . ." I let that hang.

"What about an announcer job. Surely that wouldn't put too much of a strain on you?"

I couldn't tell if Sally was busting my chops. I didn't think so. The truth was I had a chip on my shoulder when it came to my limited abilities. I tried to study her face, but she was staring into her coffee cup. Given how tight money was I'd figured her going buggy about me losing my job. Instead she'd gone quiet and sad, which was worse.

I told her nobody was going to hire me as an announcer, and they certainly weren't going to hire me for anything in front of the camera. My voice was high-pitched, a little squeaky even. On top of that I was short, 5 foot 3 inches to be exact, had chubby cheeks and looked much younger than my thirty-one years. I also walked with a pronounced limp. Those qualities made me perfect for playing a goofball of indeterminate age like Little Putt-Putt, who spent most of his time sitting down or hovering with his jet-pack. Not so much for other roles.

When I was starting out I'd been told I looked a lot like Mickey Rooney. I thought for sure that meant the work would come rolling in. To the surprise of no one but me, it turned out there was surprisingly little demand for a Mickey Rooney knock-off. The biggest part I ever got was in a Monogram quickie called The Ghost of the Voodoo Ape. I played John Carradine's dim-witted lackey who gets killed fifteen minutes into the picture. Mostly I worked as an extra in crowd scenes. Usually what happened was, the director would tell me my height was a distraction, push me further and further into the crowd until you couldn't see me at all. Like I was never there. I'm not even in the movies I'm in.

This was before the war, before I acquired the limp. After the war I didn't work at all until Ernie got me the part of Little Putt-Putt.

Sally had gotten it into her head that the show would be a stepping stone to bigger parts and happier days.

What she didn't understand was that nobody was going to hire a crippled shrimp with a bad ticker. Nobody except an old Army buddy like Ernie. I understood all too well that Little Putt-Putt was going to be my biggest and final role. I just never had the heart to tell Sally. Now that it was clear the bigger apartment wasn't in the cards, or the new car, or, worst of all, the baby, she was beginning to figure it out on her own. Watching it happen was a daily ration of heartbreak.

Her patience was like a bottomless well and it just made me feel worse. I wished she would lose her temper, give me a reason to get mad in return. She never did.

Sally moved her chair around to sit beside me, rested her head on my shoulder. She said, "We'll be okay. I can find work. I saw the laundry down the block is hiring."

When she spoke I felt her hot breath on my neck and it raised goose-bumps. Sally brought her hand up, ran her fingers through my hair. I took her by the shoulders and kissed her, and she kissed me back, both her hands on my face, pulling me closer. We were both breathing hard now, fumbling with buttons and zippers and clasps. I told myself it would be different this time. And for just a moment I believed it, thought maybe something good could come of this day after all. A few seconds later I felt the sharp pain in my chest, Yobo giving me a little nip, reminding me why Sally and I hadn't tried this in over a year. Yobo was a jealous bitch.

I pulled away quickly, gasping. Sally didn't say anything, we'd been through this too many times for words to matter anymore. She hurried into the bathroom, buttoning up her dress as she went, and shut the door behind her. Judging by her expression I suspected maybe her patience was finally running out.

I leaned against the back of the chair, taking shallow breaths, rubbing at my chest, thinking that maybe this was the night Yobo would finally go all the way. It wasn't. As usual, she was all tease and no action.

3

It was rare that I dreamed of my time in the Army, but that night, I did. The memories of my eight months in Korea were so fragmented and hazy it would have been easy to convince myself I'd never even been if it wasn't for my damaged leg. And the little piece of shrapnel in my chest.

Most of what came back to me in dreams were faces. The driver of our jeep bragging about how well he drove on those mountain roads just before the explosion flipped us. Ernie saying my name, telling me I was all right, his face bloody, his hands pressing down hard on my chest. My CO, showing a lot of teeth, telling me about the Purple Heart in my future.

The doctors were able to patch me up pretty good. Better than a lot of guys, like that jeep driver for instance. That single sliver of metal in my chest though, so sharp and so deep, they couldn't reach. Too dangerous they said, too close to my heart. Not that leaving it was much safer. They said it would shift over time, that it would slowly, but inevitably, work its way deeper.

Carrying it inside me every day, it was impossible not to be conscious of it, to know that I was living on borrowed time. I took to thinking of it as a mercurial lover holding a dagger to my heart. Moody, unpredictable, dangerous. Ready and willing to carry me into the dark, at any moment. My little sweetheart. My little Yobo.

The ringing of the bedside phone pulled me abruptly from my dreams. I looked at the clock as I picked up the phone, saw it was after midnight.

"Yeah?"

"Scotty? This is Rick. I need to see you right away."

"Christ. Are you drunk?" He didn't sound drunk, he sounded nervous.

"No kidding, Scotty, this is an emergency."

"We don't even work together anymore," I said. "Call somebody else."

The phone was halfway to its cradle when Rick said something that made me put the receiver back to my ear.

"What was that?"

Rick said again, "It's Ernie. He's dead."

4

I'd expected Sally to ask a lot of questions about where I was going at almost one in the morning, but she never even stirred. I guessed she'd taken one of the sleeping pills she typically reserved for times when the pain in my leg made me restless. I thought about leaving a note, telling her where I'd gone, but decided against it. I didn't plan on being out long.

It was raining lightly when I stepped out of our building onto the sidewalk. I tucked the folded pants and shirt under my arm, pulled my overcoat tight around me, and started across the street to the dark lot where I parked our car.

I'd dialed Ernie's number right after I got off the phone with Rick and got no answer. That's what got me up and out in the middle of the night. I owed it to Ernie.

I got in the car and was pleased when the old crate started after only three tries. I saw it as a sign that maybe my luck was turning around. As I exited the lot, a black-and-white pulled up to the curb, cutting me off and forcing me to hit the brakes. The car died.

I shot nasty looks at the cops while I attempted to start the engine again. The one in the passenger seat looked like he was having some bad luck of his own. He had an angry looking shiner, his right eye purple and swollen in my headlights. Tussling with some drunk was my guess. I wondered what kind of night the drunk was having.

The longer I sat there the madder I got. I counted slowly to ten, intent on keeping myself calm so as not to get Yobo stirred up. I turned the key again. It took six tries to fire up the engine this time. The cop with the black eye stared at me as I drove away, and I wished him a headache.

The streets were empty, and Rally's Diner was only a couple miles from my apartment, so I made it there in under fifteen minutes. I parked on the street, went in. The place was empty except for the fry-cook, a lone weary waitress, and Rick sitting in a back-corner booth. He waved me over. I could see he was still wearing his Rocket Ryder coveralls, complete with the United World Space Patrol insignia over his heart.

I sat, handed Rick the pants and shirt he'd requested. He took them, said, "They're wet."

"It's raining," I said.

"You could have put them in a bag."

"I could have stayed in bed."

"Maybe just stuck them under your coat."

"Or stick them up your ass. I don't really give a damn you have to wear wet clothes. You want to tell me what's going on?"

Rick stood up fast enough to make me nervous and I instinctively slid my hand inside my coat pocket, gripped the army issue .45 I'd brought along. It was my only wartime souvenir, aside from Yobo.

Rick said, "Let me change first. Hold on a minute."

Rick carried the pants and shirt into the men's room. I sat waiting, considering the possibility that he would climb out the bathroom window and run off. The waitress came by with a hot cup of coffee and a minute later Rick came back to the table with the wadded up coveralls in his hand.

The white button-up shirt was a good two sizes too small and stretched around Rick's broad chest, making little puckered open spaces between the buttons. The pants fit poorly as well. They were so short they stopped just above the tops of his socks, revealing his red plastic Rocket Ryder booties. Worse still, they were so tight I could see the outline of his dick. It looked like someone trying to vacuum seal an anaconda. One more thing to resent the son of a bitch for.

Rick tugged at the shirt collar and said, "Didn't you have anything bigger?"

"I usually buy clothes in my own size," I said. "And you know what they say about beggars. They should take what they fucking get."

"Fine. Let's go."

"Where?"

"Doesn't matter, long as we're moving."

"I'm not going anywhere until you tell me what happened to Ernie."

Rick glanced toward the door, said, "I'll tell you everything in the car. I just don't feel safe sitting here."

I got up, said, "You're paying for my coffee."

"With what? Did you leave money in these pants?"

I sighed, threw some change down.

Rick said, "I had some toast while I was waiting on you."

I glared at him.

Rick said, "What? I don't carry a wallet in my costume."

I tossed a dollar bill down on the table. We passed the waitress on our way out and she wished us a good night. I noticed her admiring gaze fixed on Rick's crotch. Apparently even the ridiculous clothes he had on weren't enough to distract from his appeal. I had to resist the urge to punch him in the back of the head.

5

In the car, heading down a dark road, Rick said, "That's a raw deal about the show. I thought we had a few more years. You want to know what bothers me the most? I mean, aside from being unemployed?"

"If I say no will you keep it to yourself?"

Rick ignored me. "Thing that bothers me most is we'll never know how the story ends. That bugs me. I bet it bugs the audience too. We want to know what happens to Ryder and Putt-Putt."

"I don't know about Little Putt-Putt, but I can tell you now, Rocket Ryder's going to end up face down in a ditch by the side of the road if he doesn't tell me what the fuck is going on."

"Hey, I'm the one who's having the shitty night here. Why the fuck do you think I called you?"

"Because we're such boon companions?"

"No, asshole. It's because I know you cared about Ernie as much as I did. He looked out for me same as you. He's the reason I got this job in the first place. If it wasn't for him I'd probably still be making smokers."

"You made stag films?"

"Only a few, when I was broke. They don't pay much, but at least you're getting laid. Although sometimes, kind of girls they get, that's not really a bonus. There were a couple times I would've bet money I was fucking a shaved bear. And specialty reels, like orgies and whatnot? They're a real pain. You ever do it with two women at once?"

I admitted I had not.

"Well, it's exhausting. And three women? That just gets weird."

"Is this going somewhere?"

"Just letting you know where I'd be, what I'd be doing, if it wasn't for Ernie. After we wrapped the last show I went to the dressing room, couldn't bring myself to leave right away. It was more than losing the job. The idea that we were leaving Ryder and Putt-Putt out there, drifting in space, it bothered me. I can't believe it doesn't bother you."

"We can make up our own ending later," I said. "For now just stay on track."

Rick nodded. "So I stayed behind after everyone else left. When Ernie found me he said he'd take me home. I was pretty bombed by that point and he didn't want me driving. On the way to my house Ernie says he needs to make a stop, see some guy. I figure it's somebody he owes money to. You know Ernie and his gambling. Always up to his neck. I tell him to do what he needs to do, then I climb in back to sleep it off. I'm out cold in no time. Next thing, a noise wakes me up. It's night now, dark in the backseat and I can hear voices."

Rick was staring down at the floorboard, his voice low, softer than normal, describing what he was seeing in his head. I wanted to hurry him along, tell him to get on with it. I kept quiet instead, afraid if I interrupted he'd start telling me about his sex life again.

"When I sit up I can see we're in some back-alley, no one around but the three people in front of the car, in the headlights. One of them is Ernie, down on his hands and knees, shot I think. Pretty sure the gunshot's what woke me. One of the guys is yelling at the other one, telling him he's crazy. The other one, the one with the gun in his hand says, 'Fuck this guy. He doesn't have it, so what do we need him for?' Then he shoots Ernie in the back of the head."

Rick went silent. The hiss of the tires rolling over wet pavement filled the car, sounding like a record player's needle spinning on dead wax. After a lengthy pause Rick went on.

"I thought I was going to shit myself, Scotty, I was so scared. All I could think to do was lay back down and hope like hell those two didn't spot me. I could hear them moving around, getting closer, talking about putting the body— putting Ernie in the trunk. Then I hear them at the back of the car saying how they need the keys. That's when I decided I'd better move. The one guy comes around and opens the driver's door, leans in so he can reach the ignition. I hit that bastard so hard his kids are gonna be born with headaches. I bet he can't even see out of that eye now."

I said, "You done bragging on yourself? How hard you can punch?"

Rick said, "Just letting you know I got in my licks, that's all. After that I hot-footed it out of there. Crept around in the shadows for a while till I was sure I'd lost them. Then I made it to Rally's and called you."

"Why call me? Why didn't you go to the cops?"

"That's the thing," Rick said. "Why I'm so scared. Those guys? The ones who shot Ernie? They were cops."

I flashed on a surly face staring from the window of a black-and-white, one eye badly bruised. I yanked the wheel and the tires slid on the rain-slicked street as we made a sudden U-turn. Rick's head bounced off the window with a heavy thump and he yowled in pain. I stomped the gas, sped toward home, knowing in my gut I was too damn late.

6

Tires squealed as I took a corner too fast and skidded on the wet road. I could see our building just a few blocks ahead. Even with me running every traffic light and stop sign on the way, the drive from Rally's to my place took an eternity. The cop car was still parked across the street, but now it was empty. I pulled to the curb and stopped, had one foot on the sidewalk when Rick grabbed my arm.

"If they're waiting for us, we ought to go slow and quiet."

I pulled my arm free and said, "We'll have to settle for quiet."

I got out of the car, hurried into the building and up to our fourth floor apartment. Even with my bum leg I beat Rick. I could hear him coming along behind me, struggling to keep up.

When I reached our apartment I stopped, checked the knob. Unlocked. Our door opened onto the kitchen, and I stepped inside, slowly, cautiously. The lights were on, Sally's old typewriter sitting on the kitchen table, a sheet of paper hanging limply over the keys like a wilting houseplant.

Moving quietly I went to the bedroom. Where I'd left Sally, and where I found her now. She lay face down on the bed, blankets bunched up at her feet. She wasn't breathing, and her head sat at an unnatural angle.

As I stood there looking at Sally I heard the toilet flush in the bathroom behind me. A voice called out from behind the closed door, "Goddamn, Dwayne. 'Bout time. You have to grow the beans yourself?"

I moved over, stood beside the door, my back against the wall. As I stood there something dangling from the ceiling caught my eye. Two of my ties were strung together and hung from an overhead pipe like a makeshift noose.

The bathroom door opened and a cop stepped out, head down, fooling with his zipper, still talking. He said, "I got that note written like you wanted. But I don't know that pipe is gonna hold his weight."

He gave the zipper a quick yank, and looked up just as I brought the .45 around, backhanded him hard across the face. The gunsight raked a bloody furrow in his forehead and the cop yelled out, his hands going to his face. I brought the butt of the gun down on the back of his head and he fell to his knees. I pressed the barrel against his head. My finger tightened on the trigger.

"Hold up." Rick stood in the doorway. His eyes went from the cop, to Sally's body, to me. He said, "I'll take care of him. You've got something else needs your attention."

The cop looked up, relief on his blood covered face. He thought he'd been saved. He was wrong.

Rick reared back and kicked him in the chin, sent his head bouncing back and forth like a speed-bag. He grabbed the cop by the front of his shirt and dragged him into the kitchen, commenced to beating on him.

I sat on the edge of the bed, put a hand on Sally's cooling shoulder, let it rest there for a moment. I wanted to hold her close, kiss her lips, but I couldn't bring myself to turn her over. Too afraid of what I might see in her eyes. Fear? Anger? Recrimination? All of them were justified. And any one of them would have ended me on the spot.

They had come here looking for Rick. Or me, hoping I could lead them to him. Instead they found Sally. They had killed her, by accident or design, and planned to string me up and frame me for it. I figured the paper in the typewriter to be my suicide note.

It was sloppy. A half-assed job that would have landed anyone else in the electric chair. Anyone except a couple of cops.

Rick stepped back into view, but didn't enter the room. He said, "I think I'm done with this guy. What do we do now?"

I didn't have a clue. I sat with Sally a moment longer. It seemed to me I should be sadder than I was, maybe cry and scream. Instead, a numbness crept over me, muting everything. Maybe that's natural. Maybe the serious grief would come in the days that followed. Maybe. But I knew I didn't have that kind of time.

Rick came further into the room, stood by my side, waiting for me. Finally I got up from the bed, covered Sally with the blanket. That's when we heard the front door open.

When we stepped out of the bedroom the second cop, Dwayne, was looking down at his partner sprawled on the floor, his head twisted almost completely around. His eye was swollen shut, just like Rick had predicted. Dwayne had a cardboard drink carrier holding two cups of coffee balanced on the palm of one hand, a white paper sack clutched in the other. At the sight of Rick and me, Dwayne's good eye bugged out like someone had squeezed him in the middle.

As the three of us stood staring at one another I felt a heat creeping slowly through me. The numbness that had settled over me was melting away, leaving a low simmering fury in its place. It wasn't the sudden rush of anger that would disturb Yobo and send searing pain through my chest. This was something else, something deeper, stronger, with more violent purpose. This was something my little Yobo approved of.

Dwayne opened his mouth, took a breath as if about to speak. I found myself wondering what he would say, this man who went out for donuts and coffee after murdering my wife.

Whatever he'd intended to say, he didn't. Instead he hurled the drink carrier and made a break for the door. I ducked, heard Rick scream as the hot coffee struck him. I rushed to the hallway. Dwayne was running down the stairs, taking them three at a time. I'd expected him to go for his gun, but he must have figured running was a better bet. He was almost to the bottom when I shot him twice in the back.

Rick was wiping at his face with a dish towel when I came back inside the apartment. His shirt was soaked with coffee and his scalded pink skin showed through the damp material.

Rick looked down at the cop, said, "You think he's dead?"

"Hell yes," I said. "His head's on backwards."

Rick said, "What about the other one?"

"We don't need to take his pulse either."

Rick was still staring at the body on the floor. "I didn't mean to beat on him so much. But once I started I couldn't stop. I started remembering how scared they made me feel, what they did to Ernie."

I went to the kitchen table, pulled the paper out of the typewriter. Like I thought, it was my suicide note. Corny stuff about disappointment, heartache, needing it to end. Melodramatic as hell, but not bad really. Better than the dialogue on our show. I wadded it up and threw it on the floor.

Heading down the hall, Rick and I passed by half a dozen faces peering from partially open doors. We descended the stairs in silence. I felt Rick glance at me as he stepped over Dwayne's body, but he didn't say anything. We didn't speak as we crossed the dark street, the click of our heels the only sound. We were almost to the car when we heard the sirens.

7

We were only a few blocks from my apartment when we passed a police car going in the opposite direction, siren wailing. Rick and I didn't rate a second glance. I figured we had maybe another half hour before that changed, and every cop in the city was gunning for us.

I could feel Rick watching me as I drove. He wanted to talk, sympathize with my loss. I didn't want to hear it. It was the same as when I got out of the hospital. People wanting to tell me how bad they felt about my misfortune.

When he couldn't take the silence anymore Rick said, "You okay?"

"Peachy."

Silence, then-

"Hey, Scotty?"

"Yeah?"

"We... we just killed two cops."

"They had it coming."

"Yeah, I know. But is anybody else going to believe that?"

"Doubt it. When it comes to doling out shootings and beatings, cops like to have a monopoly. They don't give a shit their buddies were crooked."

Rick said, "Wish I hadn't beat on that one so much. Should've kept my head."

I said, "Pretty sure you did him in with that first kick. The rest of it was just gravy."

Rick smacked his window, stomped his foot on the floorboard. "Shit. I don't think I'm cut out to do time."

I gave Rick a pat on the shoulder, said, "Don't worry about it. We'll never see the back of a police car."

"No?"

"No. They're going to kill us on sight."

Rick's eyes widened, then he hurriedly rolled his window down, leaned out and puked. He wiped his mouth, leaned his head against the door and let the wind muss his hair.

The sky was turning a hazy pink with the rising of the sun. More cars on the streets now, more eyes to spot us once the word was out. We needed to get off the road, find a place we could lay low, figure our next move.

I said as much to Rick and he said, "Go to Ernie's."

"You think it's safe?"

Rick shrugged. "Safer than staying out in the open. And Ernie's not likely to complain."

Ernie lived in a craftsman not far from the station. The sun was fully up by the time we got there, but his block was quiet, nobody out yet to notice us. I pulled around back to the detached garage, figuring to stash my car inside it. When I parked, raised the big door, I saw Ernie's car in there.

Rick, standing beside me, said, "That shouldn't be here. I bet those cops brought it back."

"No shit. You expect a cigar for that deduction?"

Rick said, "Don't get pissy. Maybe you're used to this kind of thing, Mr. War Hero, but I'm not. I'm rattled, and I'm trying to figure out what the fuck is going on."

I let the war hero crack slide, started searching around in the garage. After a minute I found a big tarp, threw it over my car. Next we checked the back door. It was locked, so Rick went back to the garage, found a pry-bar. He jimmied the door open with a minimum of noise and we slipped inside.

The house was trashed, chairs and tables overturned, drawers removed and upended, shelves emptied, their contents scattered on the floor. We found Ernie in the kitchen. He was propped up in a chair, his head leaning forward so that his chin rested on his chest. The back of his head was a matted bloody mess. A .38 lay on the floor beside the chair like it had fallen from his hand.

Rick picked up a typewritten sheet of paper from the table. He scanned it quickly, set it back down.

"Suicide note?"

Rick nodded.

"I give those boys no points for originality. Seems like they only had one trick up their sleeve."

Rick said, "Those bastards shot him twice. How did they plan on explaining the second bullet?"

"He missed his head the first time?"

Cold-blooded as it sounds, we decided we needed to eat. The two of us were running on nothing but adrenaline, and Rick was still looking a little green around the gills. I scrounged around in the ice-box and came up with some bologna and white bread, half a tomato.

Rick sat at the table while I made sandwiches. After a minute he said he couldn't take it anymore. He grabbed the edge of the tablecloth, whipped it off the table like a magician, and draped it over Ernie.

I put the food on the table, glanced at Ernie's shrouded form. I said, "That's supposed to be better?"

"Least he's covered up."

We both sat, sandwiches in our hands, our eyes drawn to Ernie. The way the sheet hung on him, Ernie looked like a spook-show attraction. Rick agreed it was a little on the disturbing side. Without further discussion we both got up and carried our food to the living room. Since the couch cushions were shredded we sat on the floor.

"I can't figure it," I said. "Why come to my place?"

Rick, his mouth full, said, "They thought you could lead them to me."

"How did they know who you were? How did they know who I was? It just doesn't make any sense."

Rick thought for a moment. "I was wearing my costume back in the alley, maybe they saw it, made the connection."

I finished my sandwich, mulled things over as I chewed my last bite. It still didn't set right with me. The pieces didn't fit in a way I liked.

I said, "So these two cops see you in costume, running away, in the dark no less, and they recognize you as Rick Tanner, the actor who plays Rocket Ryder on a station almost no one can pick up. So they figure, let's go ask the guy who plays his partner on the show. That seem sensible to you?"

Rick said, "Sensible or not, it's what happened."

"But why would they think you'd come to me for help? If they knew much about either of us, they'd know we can barely stand one another. Something made me the most likely person you would turn to, but I can't figure it. Aside from the show, what do we have in common?"

Rick said, "Ernie."

I thought about it, turned it this way and that in my head. I couldn't argue with the logic. We both owed our jobs to Ernie. He'd helped us both up when we were scraping bottom. It made a certain sense.

"What did that cop say? Just before he shot Ernie?"

"He said Ernie didn't have it."

"Have what?"

"The fuck should I know?"

I gestured at the messy room, said "Whatever 'it' is, looks like those two came back here to find it before they went to my place. So whatever Ernie had that they were interested in, it must still be here."

Rick put the uneaten half of his sandwich down. "How do you figure? Maybe they found it."

I shook my head. "If they'd found what they were after, they wouldn't have come looking for me."

"Why not? They still needed to find me. I was a witness."

"Maybe they weren't worried about that," I said. "They're cops, respected members of the community. You're an actor. And a damn drunk."

"Hey—"

"Don't get sensitive. I'm just saying how they saw it. If it came down to your word against theirs? If you were the only witness, I doubt those two needed to lose a wink of sleep over it. No, whatever Ernie had that was so important, that's what they came to my place for."

Rick stood up, brushed the bread crumbs from the front of his coffee stained shirt. He said, "Let's find it then."

8

It didn't take us long to find what we were looking for.

The cops had done a lousy job of searching the place. Sure, they'd looked inside, under and behind everything in the house. But they were used to looking for things that had been hidden hastily by desperate people. Ernie had been neither of those. Whatever he had that they wanted, he'd had time to hide it carefully.

Rick said, "They dumped his files on the floor."

We were in Ernie's study. It was just as torn up as the living room, desk drawers dumped out and tossed aside, shelves cleared. A small filing cabinet sat in the corner, its two drawers open, empty manila envelopes piled up next to it, papers scattered all around.

I looked at the mess, said, "Yeah? So?"

Rick said, "So it means whatever we're looking for would fit in one of those envelopes. Probably a document, or photograph or something. Makes sense, right? They wouldn't be looking for a bag full of money inside an envelope."

I had to agree with him. Not that I liked to give him credit for much, but Rick wasn't half stupid when he was sober.

I went back to the living room where I'd seen several photo albums carelessly thrown in the corner. I picked one up, flipped through it. If it was a document we were searching for maybe Ernie had hidden it behind a picture. There were a lot of them though, and I quickly realized it would take us forever to peel each one of them back and look behind it.

The last photo in the album I held was one of Ernie and me in our uniforms, leaning on a couple of shovels. It was a tad blurry. Ernie had handed his brownie to some passing grunt and made him take our photo. The man had not put his best effort into it.

In the picture it's almost nightfall, the sun just visible over the mountain tops, Ernie and me waving at the camera, wearing big smiles like we're having ourselves a grand old time instead of digging a fucking latrine in the bitter cold Korean winter.

The picture had been taken my first day there. After the months spent on my training and travel I was dumped in the Kumwha Valley, handed a shovel and told to 'go dig a shitter'. There were no permanent structures in the camp, just row after row of tents in all shapes and sizes. It was like a carnival, except there was no cotton candy, no trained animals, and the only prize you were likely to win was a bullet you didn't see coming.

With no additional instructions forthcoming I wandered up and down the rows. Finally, on the edge of camp, about twenty yards from the last row of tents I saw another soldier standing near a shallow hole, his shovel upright, the blade buried in the frozen ground.

Like most everyone else in camp, the man was wearing his heavy parka. Unlike most, he had his hood up, zipped to the neck. I couldn't see his face, only the glowing cherry of his cigarette and a faint trail of smoke drifting from the cinched mouth of the hood. He stood with one foot on the edge of the shovel blade, staring down at the hole he was digging.

It wasn't much of a hole. It didn't look to me like he'd taken more than two or three scoops of dirt before he'd stopped, and he didn't seem in a hurry to get back to it. He just stood there smoking as I approached.

"You digging a latrine?" I asked.

"Yep," the man said without looking up.

"Something interesting down there?" I asked.

"Nope. Just figuring on how long I can make this job last."

I said, "Seems like an unpleasant job. I'd think you would want to get it done as soon as possible."

The man shook his head. At least I assumed he did. I still couldn't see his face, but there was a rustling sound from inside the parka's hood, and the stream of smoke wavered from side to side.

The man said, "You finish one job, they give you another. And that next one might be the one that gets you killed. No, you get a job that doesn't involve being shot at, you drag that fucker out."

That was the most sensible thing anyone had said to me since they'd shaved my head. I stepped to the other side of the tiny hole, stabbed my shovel into the ground and adopted a similar pose to his.

I said, "I'll let you set the pace, oh wise one. They sent me to help you dig."

Ernie looked up then, cigarette dangling from his crooked smile, and said, "Well, if I knew you were coming I'd've baked a cake."

We shook hands, introduced ourselves, and took all damn day digging that hole. Ernie had the picture taken at sundown to celebrate the occasion. Later the CO reamed our asses for taking so long. He sent us back out the next day to finish the job, and we managed to drag that out until after lunch. And that was how I met Ernie.

I closed the album and stood looking around the mess in the living room. Most all of the shelves had been cleared, everything knocked to the floor. Ernie's records still sat upright in their rack near the stereo cabinet. I called Rick in from the other room.

"You find something?" he asked.

"Maybe. Who sings '*If I Knew You Were Coming I'd've Baked a Cake*?"

"That's what's on your mind right now? I don't think—"

"Goddamnit, who sings the song?"

Rick thought for a moment, said, "Barton something-or-other. Ellen?"

"Eileen. But Ernie always said she was a square. Who's the other woman?"

Rick just stared at me. Then I remembered. Georgia Gibbs sang the version Ernie liked.

Ernie was an organized man, so it only took a few seconds to go through his alphabetized collection and find the

Gibbs 78. I slid the record out, turned the sleeve over and shook it. A thin envelope fell out and fluttered to the floor.

9

I picked up the envelope, held it. Rick and I stood silently, just looking at it. It was business size, flimsy and light.

Rick said, "Doesn't seem like something worth dying for should fit in there."

Another surprising observation from Rick. He was right. Whatever was inside felt insubstantial compared to the damage it had caused. I hesitated before opening it, reminded myself that seeing what was inside was just the next step. Any answers would just lead to more questions, any explanations would be unsatisfactory. The contents, no matter what they were, were bound to disappoint in the moment.

Turned out I was wrong. The four photographs in the envelope did, in fact, lead to more questions, but they in no way disappointed. The first picture showed Dominic Vincitore in bed with two women. One woman had hold of his wrinkled old dong, stretching it out like a piece of dick-shaped taffy, while the other one crouched behind him. Dom had a big smile on his face, an unlit cigar clenched between his teeth, and instead of one of the fine, bespoke suits he was known for wearing, he had on—

"Is he wearing a slip?" Rick asked.

"Appears to be. Satin from the look of it."

"He ever light that damn cigar?"

"Not that I've ever seen."

Rick leaned in a little, peered at the picture, said, "What's that being shoved up his ass?"

"Can't tell from this angle."

The question was answered in the next picture. It was the business end of a funnel.

"I think you can put those away now," Rick said.

"You're the one likes to know how stories turn out. Don't you want to find out what they pour into the funnel?"

"Not if I live to be a hundred."

I wasn't that keen on seeing the next picture in the sequence myself. I began to stuff them back into the envelope when Rick told me to hold on, took it from my hands.

"Now you want to see what comes next?"

Rick shook his head, said, "No, I thought I saw something. Look here."

Someone had written in ink on the back of one of the pictures. The message said, Maybe you can make use of these.

"What do you suppose that means?" Rick asked.

I didn't know. But I intended to find out. I recognized the handwriting, had seen it on every one of my paychecks for the last two years. It belonged to our producer.

I said, "Let's go see Lyle."

10

We took Ernie's car and left my beater behind in the garage. It seemed like the prudent thing to do, the cops were bound to be looking for us by now.

Before we left, Rick changed back into his Rocket Ryder uniform, said the coffee smell from his shirt was starting to gag him. For my part, I was just happy not to have to look at his dick anymore. I'd been starting to worry that it might bust out of those pants and strangle me.

The Vincitore family, Lyle included, lived in a big house in a wealthy neighborhood called Mission Hills, way on the other side of town from where Ernie, Rick and I lived. I'd gone there with Sally for a Christmas party the year before. It was supposed to have been a KCTO event, but mostly it turned out to be Dom's rich friends, with a few of the staff from the station hugging the walls like dateless sad-sacks at a high school dance. The party had been a bore, and seeing that big house, all those fancy clothes, had depressed Sally. She wasn't, by nature, overly materialistic, but being around that kind of money can mess with a person's thinking, make them feel like less than they are.

I pushed my thoughts of Sally down deep, swallowing all my feelings, trying to keep everything together for just a little longer. I looked over at Rick in the passenger seat. He was staring straight ahead, his face serious.

"Something on your mind?" I asked. "I mean, something other than all this?"

"I'm just wondering what we're doing," Rick said.

"We're going to confront Lyle about those pictures."

"So do we think Lyle had Ernie killed? Or was it Dominic?"

"That's what we're going to find out. With any luck, they'll both be home."

Rick still looked troubled, "And then what? We going to kick in the door and hold them at gunpoint?"

"Yes and yes," I said. "Whatever it takes to get to the bottom of this. Those cops were the triggermen. Just doing what they were told. I want the men who told them. I want the person who set it all in motion."

"The bottom of what? We already killed the men responsible."

I realized I was tensing up, stomping down on the accelerator. I let up off the gas a little. I didn't want a simple traffic stop to put an end to my revenge seeking.

Rick said, "Maybe we have a better chance if we turn ourselves in. We have those pictures now. They're evidence. We can get our story out there, hope somebody believes it."

I pounded my hand on the steering wheel and Yobo gave me a little poke just to remind me she was along for the ride. I didn't care, I was too furious. My feelings about Sally, and Ernie and, if I'm being honest, some self-pity too, all swirled around in my head.

"We're not turning ourselves in," I said. "At least I'm not. You can do what you want. Those rich bastards ruin lives on a daily basis, and now they've ruined ours. They're going to pay for it this time. I'm going to make them pay. And before you make up your mind to stay or go, you should know this. I aim to collect the full goddamn price."

Rick just shrugged, as if he'd suddenly lost interest in the conversation. He looked worn out, his eyes sunken and weary. He sighed like he was deflating, slid low in his seat and leaned his head back. He was still like that a couple minutes later when I came to a red light.

There was a burger joint on the corner next to us, and standing outside on the curb was a small boy with his mother. The woman wore a bright yellow dress and hat, and looked like a ray of summer morning come to life as she stood rooting through her purse for change for the meter. Watching the two of them, I couldn't help but think of Sally and the life she'd wanted for us.

The boy cocked his head and stared into Rick's window. It took a moment, but I realized what he was looking at. Rocket Ryder, big as life, sitting right beside me.

I was about to tell Rick to slide lower in his seat when a cop strolled out of the diner and approached the woman. For a moment I thought it was over, but the cop was more interested in the woman, and her legs, than in us. As they chatted he dug a coin out of his pocket and handed it to her.

I told myself not to panic. We were in Ernie's car and there was no reason for the cop to even notice us. All we had to do was stay calm. I looked straight ahead and tried to feign a casual attitude.

This goddamn light was taking forever.

I spared a glance at the cop. The kid's gaze shifted from Rick to me, and I saw all doubt vanish from his eyes. He knew my chubby face in an instant, knew I was Little Putt-Putt, even out of my Space Patrol uniform. My palms grew sweaty on the steering wheel. It was strange to think that only 24 hours ago being recognized would have been the highlight of my day.

The boy opened his mouth, no doubt to point us out to his mother. I put a finger to my lips, then made a fist and placed it to my forehead. The Space Patrol Salute. The boy smiled, and returned the salute.

The light changed and it was all I could do not to burn rubber getting away from there. As we drove away I glanced in the rearview mirror. The boy and his mother were walking away, the cop ogling her as she went, not so much as a glance in our direction.

Rick still sat with his head back, only now he'd closed his eyes. He didn't open them again until we reached the Vincitore mansion.

11

I had been worried about getting through the front gate, but my worry turned out to be for nothing because the gate stood wide open. I suppose when you're as connected as Dominic Vincitore, common type intruders aren't a concern.

I passed through the gate and up the long, crushed-gravel drive. Up closer to the house the drive became a paved circle with a narrower part that branched off and ran around to the back. A shiny black Cadillac El Dorado sat in the circle drive.

An old man in dark pants and rolled up shirtsleeves was out waxing the car, his hand moving a rag in tight fast circles. The man's hair was ash grey, his coffee colored skin thin and leathery. He looked up and stopped his work when he saw us coming.

Rick looked around, admiring the big house and the vast, well-tended acreage. He'd skipped the Christmas party, so this was his first exposure to the Vincitore estate.

He said, "This seems kind of anti-climactic. We just drive right up, do our thing?"

"We're not inside yet," I said. "Let's see how the next minute or two go before we declare the job done."

Rick gave a nod. He still seemed drained of energy, his responses a little slow. I hoped when the time came, and I needed him, he would pull himself together.

I pulled behind the Caddy and turned off the engine. We got out and Rick moved around the car like he was carrying something heavy on his back, his shoulders slumped, shuffling his feet. The old man watched us warily.

I said, "The Vincitores home?"

"You got an appointment? Reason I ask is, they don't usually let nobody through the door less they got an appointment."

"You their secretary?"

The man chuckled a bit at that, said, "Naw. I just take care of the cars. I was only trying to save you from getting what they call 'forcibly ejected'."

I pulled the .45 from my coat pocket, held it down by my side, said, "Let me worry about that. You just tell me are they home."

At the sight of the gun the man raised his hands, the rag still clutched in his left. He said, "Lyle's inside. Julie too. The old man and the others are gone. Anything else you want to know?"

I shook my head. "You can put your hands down."

"Uh-uh. I move too fast, you might get the wrong idea and shoot me."

Rick said, "No offense, old timer, but you don't look like you got many fast moves left in you."

"Fuck you. And your little red booties."

Rick said, "For a man so concerned about getting shot, you're awful lippy."

Clarence said. "You ain't the one with the gun."

Rick said, "I can still kick your ass."

Clarence said, "Try it, and you're like to see some of them fast moves I was talking about."

I said, "Clarence, put your hands down. I'm not going to shoot you. But I am going to have to ask you to get in the trunk."

"And I'm gonna have to ask you to kiss my colored ass."

"You are a hard man to put up with," I said.

"You ain't making no new friends here yourself," Clarence said. "I got the claustrophobic real bad. I get in that trunk, I won't be able to breathe."

I said. "You'll breathe just fine. Soon as I finish my business inside I'll let you out."

Clarence shook his head. "Uh-uh. Can't you just hit me over the head with the gun, knock me out?"

"That only works in the movies," I said. "I knock you in the head with this thing you won't know cat piss from pea soup."

"I don't care much for neither," Clarence said. "So that's no hardship. I'm telling you, I can't get in that trunk. So go on, conk me one. Just do it quick."

Clarence turned around, showed me the bald spot on the back of his head. He tapped a finger on it, like that was my target. I looked at Rick and he gave me a shrug. I really didn't want to bash an old man in the head, but I couldn't risk him running off, calling the police, while I was inside dealing with Lyle.

I said, "Okay, on three. One...two...th-"

Clarence spun around, said, "I changed my mind. Put me in the trunk. I thought you'd back down, maybe just tie me up, but you two were really gonna beat me over the head."

"Don't act like it was our idea," Rick said. "You asked us to."

"Oh, that's right," Clarence said. "I was looking in the mirror this morning thinking, my head's too round, I wish a pair of crackers would show up and put some new lumps on it, reshape it a little."

While Clarence was complaining I opened the car door, got the keys and opened the trunk. It was nice and roomy and I motioned with the gun for Clarence. He came to the rear of the car and looked in the trunk, an expression on his face like he'd just gotten bad news from the doctor. Finally, he sighed and sat on the lip of the trunk, lifted his legs up and got in, laid flat.

Clarence looked up at me and said, "You sure you're gonna let me out in a few minutes? You won't forget?"

I said, "I gave you my word."

"I've heard of white folks who keep their word. Just never met one." Clarence took a deep breath and squeezed his eyes closed.

I shut the trunk, turned to Rick and nodded toward the front door. As we walked away I heard Clarence call out, telling us to hurry the fuck up.

"So, are they home?" Rick asked.

"Just Lyle and some girl named Julie," I said. "But that's a start. If I don't like what Lyle has to say, I'm betting he can tell us where Dom is."

The front door was flanked by two tall white pillars that supported nothing. On the door was a brass knocker in the shape of a bulldog's head, a big brass bone in its mouth. The thing felt like it weighed ten pounds and I banged it against the door like I was driving nails. A few seconds went by and I hammered again, this time going on for a good thirty seconds. We waited, and I was about to give the knocker another go when I heard the click of the latch.

The door opened slowly and there was Lyle in his bathrobe, hair mussed, eyes puffy and red. It appeared we'd woken him up. Lyle and I were the same age, but he looked a good decade older. The years of drinking and carousing showed in the lines on his face and the fine web of broken blood vessels around his nose.

Lyle rubbed at his eyes, was about to say something when he all at once recognized us. He blinked several times, then screamed like a little girl and tried to throw the door shut. I hit it hard with my shoulder, pushed my way inside.

Lyle turned and ran, still wailing like an air raid siren. A telephone table sat just inside the door and the long phone cord trailed down onto the floor in a loop. Lyle's foot caught the cord, tripped him, sent him face down onto the marble floor with a whack. He lay still as blood pooled beneath his face.

"Well, that went sour fast," Rick said. "We killed him before we even got in the door."

I moved closer and knelt down beside Lyle, noticed he was still breathing. "He's not dead," I said. "So there's a bit of luck."

I turned him over and saw that his nose was mashed flat against his face, swelling up fast and turning a horrific shade of purple. One of his front teeth had been knocked out as well.

Behind me, Rick stepped inside, looked up at the high ceiling, the art on the walls, and gave an appreciative whistle. He stepped over Lyle without further comment, passed through an archway on the left into what looked like some kind of parlor. A well-stocked liquor cabinet sat against the back wall and Rick made a bee-line for it. He opened the cabinet and scanned the rows of bottles until he found something he liked, thumbed the top off, and drank from the bottle like it was tap water. I think it was scotch.

I said, "Hey, you're no help to me if I have to carry your drunk ass."

"I'll be fine," he said, throwing back another massive slug. "Just need something to take the edge off."

I had to admit, he was looking livelier than a few minutes ago. What did I care if he pickled his liver, as long as he didn't get in the way of what I needed to do.

Just then I heard someone say, "What's all the noise?"

I was standing at the foot of a long, wide staircase that curved up the wall to a second floor walkway. A man, tall, broad shouldered and bald as a river rock, was almost halfway down. He was dressed like Clarence, only his shirt was untucked and he was barefoot. It looked like we'd woken him up too.

I raised my gun, thinking to stop him in his tracks. Instead the crazy bastard leaped the last six stairs and crashed into me. We both slammed into the wall, then fell to the floor.

The gun went flying, clattered across the polished marble and slid under the telephone table.

I landed a couple of punches, but the man's head felt made of stone. He straddled me, started hitting me in the face so fast and furious the stars I saw were seeing stars.

About the time all those stars grabbed hands and began singing nursery rhymes I heard a crash, and something wet splashed my face. When my vision cleared, Rick was standing over me holding the jagged neck of the broken bottle of scotch. Baldie was on one knee, shaking his head like he expected a loose part to roll out of his ear, and his scalp looked like someone had decided it would be more attractive painted red and decorated with jagged bits of glass.

I got to my feet as Rick and Baldie squared off, my mind on retrieving the gun. Then Yobo drove the knife in. I stiffened, clutched at my chest.

I didn't want this to be the big embrace. Not now. I had too much to do. I started to plead with Yobo, beg for just a little more time, but then stopped. It felt too much like praying for my comfort.

I pushed back the pain, and whispered to Yobo, once and for all, to put out or shut the fuck up. She backed off, sulkily I imagined. I rested there against the wall, watched Rick and Baldie go to town on one another.

In that moment, watching Rick duke it out while in costume, I felt like I knew what the kids saw in him. Just then his overalls and red booties didn't look so ridiculous. He wasn't a bad acting drunk who made stag films in his spare time, he was goddamn Rocket Ryder, kicking ass and pulling Little Putt-Putt out of another jam.

Rick and Baldie were landing pile-driver punches that sounded like someone tenderizing meat. Rick would land a haymaker that would send Baldie staggering back, only to be driven backward himself when Baldie came back with a roundhouse. This went on for several exchanges, each man taking a severe beating. Baldie had about twenty pounds on Rick, and his size was proving to be the deciding factor. Rick was slowing down, still landing punches, but not as many and not as fast.

Just when it looked like Baldie had gained the upper hand, his foot came down on a piece of glass and he jerked back with a yelp, hopping on one foot. Rick put his head down and butted him hard, drove Baldie backward and slammed him into a china cabinet. Rick moved out of the way as shattered glass rained down on Baldie's face and into his open mouth.

Baldie pulled himself free of the wrecked cabinet, cutting his hands to ribbons in the process. He took a stance like he was ready for round two, before he realized he didn't have any fight left and dropped to his knees. Baldie turned his head, spit out a mouthful of what looked like red gravel, then fell forward onto his belly, a shard of glass sticking six inches out his back. Baldie tried to pull himself forward with his blood-slicked hands but could find no purchase on the marble floor. Finally he gave up, put his head down and lay still, too weak to move, his breathing coming fast and shallow.

Then the cabinet tipped forward and crashed down on top of him.

By then the pain in my chest had eased up further, allowing me breathe again. Rick came over and helped me to my feet. We looked down at the mess of splintered wood and broken glass. The only part of Baldie visible was one of his hands. The fingers twitched for a few seconds, then stopped.

"That wasn't so anti-climactic after all," I said.

Rick said nothing as he went to the liquor cabinet to find another bottle.

12

We carried Lyle to the parlor, laid him out on the couch, and Rick poured scotch over his face. Lyle gagged and coughed, finally coming around. He looked at me, uncomprehending. Not all the way awake, I decided, and I slapped him hard.

"Ow! What the fuck was that for?"

"Trying to help you wake up."

"Next time try, 'Hey, Lyle. You awake?' See if that does the trick."

"How do you know I didn't already try that," I said.

"Did you?"

"No. I pretty much slapped you first thing. And I liked it so much I'm thinking of doing it again you don't tell me what I want to know."

"No need for that," Lyle said. With his smashed-in nose he sounded like he had a bad cold.

"Who else is in the house?"

"Just me and Julius," Lyle said. He looked around at the mess, the blood-smeared floor, said, "But it looks like you already met Big Julie."

Big Julie. That figured. I wondered if Clarence had misled me on purpose or not. I decided not. If I got killed, who would know he was locked in the trunk?

"Are you guys mad about the show?" Lyle asked. "Is that why you're here? I knew you wouldn't like being replaced by Buck Rogers, but I didn't have anything to do with that. It wasn't my call. DuMont wants-"

Rick cut him off, said, "You're really going to pretend you don't know why we're here?"

"Pretend, hell," Lyle said. "I got no idea why you two morons are here."

Rick made a disbelieving noise as he took several swallows from his current bottle.

Lyle said, "That's a 25 year old Lagavulin you're guzzling."

Rick smacked his lips, said, "Turns to piss just as quick as anything else."

Lyle started to say something else and I gave his ear a painful flick, just to get his attention.

"If you don't know why we're here," I asked. "Then why'd you run when you saw us?"

"Why do you think?" Lyle said. "You two are all over the radio. Local actors on a killing spree. Not even finished with my first cup of coffee and I'm hearing about you shooting cops in the street."

"Cops you sent to my place," I said.

"I didn't expect you to kill them," Lyle said.

"But you didn't care if they killed me."

The look of confusion came back into Lyle's eyes. "I don't know what you're talking about."

Rick turned away from the conversation and wandered off deeper into the house, draining the dregs of his bottle as he went. I told him not to wander far, but he didn't answer. I turned my attention back to Lyle.

Lyle held up his hands in surrender, said, "Look, those two cops called, said they needed to find Rick."

"And did they tell you why?"

Lyle looked down at the ground. "They said Ernie was dead and that Rick was involved. I told them he might contact you, seeing how both of you were tight with Ernie, that's all. I swear I didn't send them to kill you. Why the fuck would I?"

"They're the ones who killed Ernie, you son of a bitch. Then they killed my wife."

Lyle looked suddenly pale, like he might get sick at any second. "I don't know about any of this. You have to believe me."

I was torn in that moment. Lyle seemed to be telling the truth, so far as it went. He clearly wasn't telling me everything, but he seemed genuinely surprised to hear that the cops had killed Ernie and Sally. I was tempted to get out the photos of Dom, ask how Ernie got hold of them, why Lyle's handwriting was on the back. But I wanted to save those, confront him and Dom at the same time, see if I could catch them up in their lies. As much as I wanted the two of them dead, I wanted to hear them confess first. I needed it, craved it like Rick craved booze.

"Where's Dom?" I asked.

"Gone fishing," Lyle said.

I slapped him again, hard enough to hurt my hand.

Lyle yelped, said, "I'm serious. He went on a fishing trip."

I said, "Oh. I thought you were being a wise ass."

"If you're just going to beat on me anyway, why bother asking questions?"

"I said it was a mistake. Let it go."

Lyle rubbed at his face, said, "Easy for you to say. You're not the one getting your ears boxed."

Lyle got an expression like he'd just tasted something sour. He gave me a mean stare, said, "You knocked a tooth out, goddamnit."

"I can't take credit for that," I said. "You did that when you tripped earlier."

"I tripped running from you," Lyle said. "I think you can take partial credit."

Seeing Lyle's prissy, irritated expression made me want to drag him off the couch and beat his head against the floor until it came apart in my hands. I held off, partly because I didn't think I had it in me right then, but also because I still needed Lyle, which meant his brain needed to stay inside his skull.

None of this was going the way I wanted. I'd imagined myself tearing through every obstacle on my path to revenge, fueled by my grief, unstoppable in my anger. But instead of busting down walls, every step I took was a slog through the swamp of complaints and desires of uncooperative bit players in my drama. This, along with the now constant ache in my chest, and the mixture of rage and sorrow I kept burying deeper, made me feel at war with everything and everyone. When I couldn't take another second of thinking about it, I grabbed the collar of Lyle's robe and hauled him to his feet.

As I pulled Lyle toward the door we met Rick coming back into the room. He carried a fresh bottle of scotch and a shotgun. He handed me a box of ammo for my .45.

"Found the gun cabinet," he said. "It was in the room next door to the billiard room. Because of course, the son of a bitch has a billiard room."

"Let's go," I said to Rick. I spoke softly, working to keep myself calm and thinking clearly.

"Where to?" Rick asked.

"Looks like," I said, "we're going fishing."

13

We were in the car, almost to the front gate, when I remembered Clarence in the trunk. I turned around, went back and let him out while Rick stayed in the car watching Lyle. When I opened the trunk Clarence sat up. He was covered in sweat and his hands shook as he swiped at his face with the rag he still held.

I said, "Sorry I had to do that."

"Well, that surely makes it better. Almost like it never happened."

"Fine," I said. "Be mad if you want. But if you knew what the Vincitorres have done, how many people they've hurt, you'd understand my actions."

Clarence said, "They treat me okay. Worse thing they've done is leave me off their Christmas card list, and I can live with that."

"So it doesn't matter what they do, long as they don't do it to you?"

Clarence said, "Listen to you, all full of self-righteous. I bet you weren't so down on'em till they did something to you. Am I right?"

I didn't answer.

"That's what I figured," Clarence said. "I've felt the need for revenge a time or two myself, and I can tell you there ain't no satisfaction at the end of that road."

"Maybe you and I just travel different roads."

Clarence sighed, and shook his head. "You're not hearing me. But I doubt you can hear anybody right now." He waved me away. "Go on. I don't want to talk to you no more. You done locked me in a trunk."

"Don't suppose you could hold off on calling the police?" I asked.

Clarence shook his head. "Give'em half a chance, the police are gonna blame me for this. I'll be lucky I'm not strange fruit by sundown. Best I can do, I won't look to see which way you turn at the end of the driveway."

I glanced toward the house, thought about the phone just inside the door. Even with Clarence being old I couldn't see it taking him long to get to it.

Clarence guessed my thoughts, said, "I'm not allowed to go in the front door. I got to go around back, use the phone in the garage."

I said, "Tell me again how good to you the Vincitorres are."

Clarence said, "I'll tell you this much, they never locked me in no goddamn trunk."

Without another word Clarence started up the driveway toward the back of the house. He wasn't lollygagging either, so I knew he meant it when he said he intended to call the police. I went back to the car and drove away from there.

14

Lyle told us Dom had a fishing cabin down in Warsaw and that's where he'd gone. He'd left Big Julie behind, but otherwise had taken the rest of his gun thugs with him. Six guys according to Lyle, whose certainty I didn't trust.

"I wish you would've let me put some clothes on," Lyle said. "Seeing as we're driving all the way to the lake."

"You're fine the way you are," I said. I figured without pants or shoes Lyle was less likely to try and escape.

"Why do I need to go along anyway?" Lyle asked. "I already told you I didn't have anything to do with Ernie, or your wife."

Rick said, "Maybe he doesn't entirely believe you." He was sitting sideways, his back against the door, the barrel of the shotgun resting on the seatback and pointed in Lyle's general direction.

"What do you plan to do once you get there?" Lyle asked.

Rick said, "You just sit back and enjoy the ride. Quietly."

"Well, I don't think either one of you knows what you're doing," Lyle said, then leaned back, pulled his bathrobe tighter.

Travelling with Lyle was like taking a car trip with an irritating child. He fidgeted in his seat, sighed dramatically a few times. He hummed to himself for a while until I threatened him with bodily harm, then he went sullenly quiet. After an hour or so he fell asleep, his mouth hanging open, snoring wetly.

With Lyle asleep I expected Rick to pester me about our plan, ask me for details. But he never said a word, his previous reservations gone, along with his sobriety. Drunk Rick was a nearly unmanageable asshole, but he was also game for anything. That was good, because the truth was I had no plan beyond confronting Dom with those pictures, getting some satisfying answers, finding out once and for all who to blame.

I avoided the main highway, sticking to country roads and alternate routes as much as possible even though it added to our drive. I had no reason to believe the cops were looking for Ernie's car, but better safe than shot dead.

We were well outside Kansas City, deep in the countryside on Route 13, when I pulled in to a rundown filling station that looked like it had been there since before the invention of the automobile. The pump jockey was a skinny guy with red hair and finger smears of grease on either cheek that made him resemble an Indian on the warpath. He moseyed over to the car, twisting his face all up as he came. At first I thought he was making faces at us, but when he leaned down by my window I saw he was just chewing an oversized wad of gum.

The tag on his work shirt said Clete. He looked in back at Lyle with his busted up face, sawing logs in his bathrobe, then at Rick dressed in his Rocket Ryder costume, a shotgun and a bottle of scotch resting in his lap, and finally at me. I smiled and told him to fill'er up. Clete, stone-faced and working the shit out of that gum, gave a curt nod, and set about filling the tank.

I heard Lyle stir in the backseat and turned to look at him. He raised his head, smacking his lips and looking around. His face fell as he remembered where he was, who he was with.

Lyle said, "I have to piss."

Rick and I looked at each other. I shrugged.

Rick said, "I'll take him. I kind of have to go myself."

"Okay," I said. "Just hurry up."

"It takes as long as it takes," Rick said. He got out, carrying the shotgun in one hand, opened Lyle's door and pulled him out of the car by the front of his robe.

Rick called to Clete over the top of the car, "We need to use your john. There a key?"

Clete said, "She's unlocked. Ain't nothin' to steal in a shitter."

Rick took hold of Lyle's robe collar and began towing him across the parking lot. Lyle swatted his hand away, telling Rick he wasn't a goddamn puppy so quit dragging him around by the scruff. Rick slapped him in the back of the head, grabbed his ear and pulled him behind the station, Lyle hollering all the way.

I glanced at Clete who was watching all this with the same blank-faced interest he'd shown everything else.

After a minute or so he finished filling the tank and was hanging the nozzle back on the pump when Rick reappeared. He had hold of Lyle's robe again, this time dragging him forcefully. The robe was now wet and smeared with dirt, hanging open to show Lyle's blue boxers. Lyle stumbled along as fast as he could, but the graveled lot made walking barefoot a painful chore. When they reached the car Rick opened the back door, shoved Lyle inside, then resumed his spot in the passenger seat. He picked up his scotch from the floorboard and took a long drink that emptied the bottle.

Other than telling me how much I owed, Clete never said another word. As we pulled away I looked in the rearview and saw him standing beside the pumps, watching us go, hands in his pockets. He continued to stare after us, face contorting this way and that as he chewed, until we were out of sight. Watching his gurning face recede in the distance, I couldn't help but feel I was being mocked.

15

"What happened to laughing boy back there? Why's he all wet?"

Rick said, "Bastard tried to make a run for it while I was taking a piss, fell into the creek behind the filling station."

"Fell my ass," Lyle said. "That son of a bitch knocked me into it. Hit me in the back of the head with that shotgun."

Rick nodded, said "Yeah, that's what really happened. But I like the way I tell it. Makes him sound dumber that way."

"Why does he smell so bad?" I asked.

"I'll tell you why," Lyle said. "I think that country goober back there prefers to do his business in and around that creek. I'm covered in muddy shit. Or shitty mud, however you want to see it."

It wasn't but another mile or two before I pulled over, made Lyle get out, chuck his robe in a ditch. Afterwards he climbed back in the car, hugging himself, looking beat up and miserable. I felt a twinge of guilt at treating him so badly, then I remembered why I was doing it and the guilt went away.

Another forty-five minutes on back-country roads and I had to ask Lyle for directions. He was pouting and not in the mood to help.

He said, "I can't believe you two assholes drug me all the way out here."

Rick, whose mood was turning sour now that he'd run out of scotch, said, "Keep running your mouth and I'll put you back to sleep."

"All I'm saying is, I could've written down the directions for you. I didn't need to come along."

"I want you here," I said. "What you want doesn't factor into it. Not today. Not anymore."

Lyle guided us onto a bumpy, tree-lined road, then after a few more miles, onto an even bumpier, more poorly maintained dirt road. A few minutes later I saw flashes of light through the trees on the right, the sun reflecting off the water. Lyle said his dad's place was up ahead, on the other side of the lake.

When I caught sight of the cabin I pulled off into the thick brush and parked behind a cluster of trees so the car couldn't be seen from the road. We all got out, crouched down in the shade, and I studied on the situation.

The fishing cabin sat close to the lakeshore. It was less a cabin and more a small cottage, painted white with shuttered windows, a porch swing in front, and a floating dock that bobbed and swayed on the water like a long wooden tongue. It was the sort of place I imagined Sally would've wanted. Behind the cabin was a long, low-roofed bunkhouse, the raw wood unpainted and weather-worn. I figured the house was for Dom, the other for his gun thugs. If I was right, it would make things a whole lot easier.

"I think I'm getting chiggers in my ass crack," Lyle said. "You boys mind if I sit in the car."

"Sure," I said. "You want the keys so you can listen to the radio?"

"Really?"

"Hell no," I said. "Now shut the fuck up and sit there quiet. On second thought, you still smell like shit. Go sit over there a ways."

Lyle got up and moped a few yards away, sat down with his bare back against a tree. He crossed his arms, put on a glum face, then shifted around and grunted, just so I'd know he was uncomfortable. He'd graduated from bratty child to moody adolescent, and it wasn't an improvement.

Rick gave a short laugh, said, "It's kind of nice, isn't it?"

"What's that?" I asked.

"Having somebody like him around. Somebody beneath you, y'know, to mistreat when you're of a mind."

"I'm treating him the way he deserves," I said.

Rick said, "Exactly."

Before I could say more a faint buzzing sound captured my attention. It grew gradually louder as two jon boats came into view. Dom, dressed in dungarees and a fishing vest, manned the outboard on the lead boat, which he had to himself. The second boat followed along at a slower pace. Slower because all six of his men were piled in and weighing the thing down.

Dom guided the jon boat to the dock, tied off and stepped onto the dock with his fishing pole in one hand and a line of fish in the other. The second boat banged and scraped along the opposite side, accompanied by much swearing from the men on board, before it was tied off as well. Once everyone had disembarked, Dom passed the line of fish off to one of his men, said a few words and went inside the cabin. The men threw their poles down in a haphazard pile on the shore and headed for the bunkhouse. I got the feeling they were not the most enthusiastic of fishermen.

Rick said, "What now?"

I thought a moment, said, "Now we wait. It'll be dark in about two hours-"

"Two hours?" Lyle whined.

"Shut it," I said. "We wait until dark, then go have a talk with Dom without all his gun hands around."

"I really hate to say this," Rick said, "but Lyle's right. Dom's in the cabin, his boys are in the bunkhouse. Why wait?"

I said, "There's a lot of open space between here and Dom's cabin. There's less chance we'll be spotted if we wait until dark."

Rick gave that disinterested shrug of his. Not entirely convinced, but not in the mood to argue. That was okay, I wasn't entirely convinced myself. There was a chance we'd be spotted, but really I was just hesitant to make the next move. Up until now I'd been focused on getting my hands on Lyle, then Dom. For every step I'd taken there was another still ahead. Now that I was close to reaching Dom, I couldn't see anything beyond that moment. Just a darkness, like a black curtain had fallen between me and the future.

Delaying the moment of confrontation felt right. Was I savoring the anticipation or just uncertain? I didn't know, but either way, we waited.

16

We spent two hours crouched in those bug filled weeds, and the time didn't pass quickly. As the sun went down the bugs got thicker. None of us spoke much, so the only sounds were us slapping at our necks and arms, and faint laughter from the bunkhouse across the lake. Thinking about those assholes sitting over there comfortable while we were being eaten alive by mosquitos kept me in the right frame of mind for what I figured was coming next.

Rick said, "You think it's dark enough yet?"

"I'd say it is," Lyle chimed in.

"I wasn't asking you," Rick said.

Before I could answer him the weeds around us lit up. It was a car coming down the dirt road. The light grew gradually brighter, then skimmed over us and went on by. I could hear raucous music from inside as the car zipped past.

Rick and I looked at each other, then followed the glow of the headlights as they curved around in the shadowy woods and out of sight. A few minutes later they reappeared as the car pulled up beside the bunkhouse.

The sound of car doors opening and shutting carried across the lake, along with the sound of female voices hooting and laughing. Hookers, I figured, and probably getting paid a pretty penny to drive way out here in the sticks. The door to the bunkhouse opened and one of the men stepped out onto the porch, ushered the women inside. I watched their silhouettes and counted five of them. I wondered for a moment how that was going to play out for the six men inside. I felt a momentary pang of sympathy for the poor bastard condemned to going stag that night.

"Now?" Rick asked.

I told him yes, and then we loaded Lyle in the backseat and drove around the lake. To be certain we weren't spotted, I turned the headlights off long before we got near the cabin, then parked a quarter of a mile down the road and walked the rest of the way in. We herded Lyle in front of us as we made our way. He complained about walking barefooted, but a kick in the ass from Rick shut him up.

"Ease up on him," I said.

I wasn't sure why I said it, but something was starting to feel wrong inside. Maybe it was what Rick had said about mistreating Lyle, or maybe it was Clarence's advice, but the closer I got to my goal, the less certain I felt about things. I ignored the thought, just like I'd done with every other troubling thought that day, and marched on.

The laughter from the bunkhouse was louder now and I felt confident that the men inside were occupied for the night. It seemed as if the arrival of the hookers had worked out in our favor.

When we got close to the cabin I motioned for Rick and Lyle to wait. I moved onto the porch, peered into the window. Inside I could see Dom seated in a cushy wingback chair, his feet up, a book in his hand, that unlit cigar in his mouth. An end table next to his chair held a mahogany humidor, along with a mason jar full of clear liquid. Dom picked up the jar and sipped from it. Moonshine, probably local, Dom's idea of slumming.

I turned back to Rick and motioned in Lyle's direction. Rick grabbed Lyle by the arm and pulled him up on the porch. I tapped a finger on my chest pointed at the door, letting him know I was going in first. Rick nodded.

I reared back and slammed my foot into the door, just to the left of the latch. The wood splintered and the door flew open and banged against the wall. I stepped in and moved aside as Rick gave Lyle a shove that sent him sprawling at Dom's feet.

Dom jumped, spilling half the jar of moonshine down his shirtfront and on his pants. He looked from Lyle to me, then back down at Lyle.

"What the hell is this?" Dom asked. Then after a second he said, "What happened to your face? And why the fuck are you in your underwear?"

Lyle said, "Ask these two morons."

Dom looked at us, finally recognizing Rick and me. He set the mason jar on the end table beside his chair, ran his hands through his thick silver hair. After considering the situation he leaned forward as if to get up.

"Stay right there," I said.

Dom hesitated, taking a good long look at the .45 in my hand and the shotgun Rick held. He leaned back in his chair, put the unlit cigar back in his mouth and tried to look relaxed as Rick shut the door and set about pulling all the blinds down.

Dom said, "Now that we're all settled in, are you going to tell me what it is you want?"

I took the envelope out of my coat pocket, tossed it onto Dom's lap. He opened it, took out the photos, flipped through them. I had to hand it to him, he stayed as cool as fresh sheets, showing no sign of embarrassment or surprise. After a brief examination he looked up at me and shrugged.

"What's this?" Dom asked. "If you're trying to blackmail me you're late to the party. Your pal Ernie already tried that."

"And you killed him for it," I said.

Dom narrowed his eyes, looked at me with suspicion. He looked down at Lyle sitting Indian-style on the floor beside his chair.

"Ernie's dead," Lyle said. "These two think I had something to do with it. Or maybe they think you did. They haven't been real clear on that."

"Turn those pictures over," I said. "Let's see if that sparks some conversation."

Dom turned the pictures face down, fanned them out across his lap. When he saw the hand-written message on the one, he scooped them up all at once and struck Lyle across the face with the whole mess.

"You little sneak-shit," Dom said. "You took these out of my album."

"You have an album for that?" Rick asked.

Dom kept his attention on Lyle, didn't even acknowledge that Rick had spoken. He couldn't have ignored us more, as if neither us, nor the fact of our guns, mattered to him.

"Why would you take these?" Dom asked. "Are you a pre-vert? Is that it? You some kind of fagola?"

"That's rich," Lyle said. "Coming from a man who likes buttermilk enemas."

Rick said softly, "Well, now we know what went in the funnel."

"If you weren't lumping your pud to these," Dom said. "Then what in the name of sweet, roller-skating Jesus were you doing with them?"

Lyle said, "I gave them to Ernie."

Dom got a look on his face I both recognized and sympathized with. It was the urge to knock Lyle upside the head. Instead, Dom took a deep breath and let it out slow.

Dom said, "Lyle, I'm not in the mood to play twenty questions with you. Now give me a straight answer or I'm going to open a boot factory in your ass."

Lyle stared at the floor in a sulk, said, "When I found out you were selling the station, cancelling the show, I stole the pictures, slipped them under Ernie's office door."

"But why?" Dom asked.

"I hate working at that goddamn place," Lyle said. "At least as a producer I hardly have to show up. But now you want me to be station manager, and to hell with that."

Dom said, "Why the fuck didn't you just say so?"

"Because," Lyle said. "you'd never let me hear the end of it. I didn't want you throwing it in my face all the time, so I gave the pictures to Ernie, figured he'd come to you, try to work a deal. And he did."

I said, "That's horse shit. Ernie didn't need the damn job that bad."

Lyle looked at me in confusion, said, "He didn't do it for himself. He did it for you, and Rocket Rumpot over there."

"What the fuck are you talking about?"

Dom said, "I can verify that part of his story. Ernie called me up, told me he had some pictures, described them in great detail. He wanted me to guarantee you and Rick would have jobs after the station sold or he was going to start showing these around."

"So that's why you had him killed," Rick said. He had moved over by the end table, picked up the mason jar. He took a long swallow, let out a whistle.

"You boys have to let go of that notion," Dom said. "I didn't have anybody killed. Those are the old days. I'm legitimate now. Or close enough for government work anyway. You think I'm worried about these pictures? If you see a picture of me in the paper it's because I want it to be seen. There isn't an editor, journalist, cop or criminal in town I can't buy or don't already own. I had no reason to kill Ernie. All I needed to do was string him along for a bit, stall him until Monday to avoid any hiccups in the DuMont deal. After that I didn't care who he showed these to."

"Was that the job you gave your pet cops?" I asked. "To stall Ernie?"

Dom said, "That's right. Stall him, that's all. You're telling me Dwayne and Carl killed Ernie?"

"And my wife," I said.

"How the hell did that happen?" Dom asked, looking to Lyle for the answer.

Lyle laid out his version of events for Dom. How Dwayne and Carl had called him looking for Rick, how Rick and I killed them both and were currently being hunted by the police, how we'd invaded the Vincitore home, killed Big Julie, and kidnapped Lyle.

Lyle ended by saying, "It wasn't my fault. Things just went south."

I said, "Things went south?"

I pointed the .45 at Lyle with a trembling hand. I was so angry I was practically vibrating. Angry at the way they kept relegating Sally's death to a footnote. Angry that all of this had been set into motion just because Lyle didn't like his job. And angry that Dom wasn't the criminal mastermind behind it all. He was only a rich, sleazy, son of a bitch.

Lyle cowered as I approached him, gun extended. I'd threatened him many times over the course of the day, but this time was different. This time he could sense I was serious, how close to death he was. Lyle held his hands up in a defensive position. A high mewling sound escaped his throat, and a wet spot spread across his crotch.

Dom said, "Hey now, there's no need for that. He didn't kill Ernie."

I glared at Dom.

"Or your wife," he added. "Dwayne and Carl, they were wild, thought they could get away with anything. And that was before I put'em on the payroll. I told them I was going to cut them loose if they didn't get their act together. In fact, this meeting with Ernie was their last chance. Why they were so desperate to cover their tracks when they fucked it up. Seems to me- and this may be hard to hear- if you killed Dwayne and Carl, you've already got all the justice you're going to get. There's nobody left to blame."

Before I could disagree, the door to the cabin burst open and one of Dom's thugs rushed inside.

17

They must have been having quite a wing-ding in the bunkhouse because the man's face was sweaty, his nose clown red, and he smelled like Rick on a Monday morning. The man's shirt was unbuttoned down to his navel and his heavily pomaded hair was mussed.

Red Nose, slurring his words, said, "Hey, Dom. You gotta come check out the trick this chickie does with a ping-pong..."

The man cut himself off as Rick and I turned to face him. He had a moment to register the weapons we held, then his hand swept past his waist and came up with a snub-nose .38. He fired.

The bullet struck Lyle in the right eye. Red Nose actually said, "Oops". Then Rick shot him in the chest with the shotgun, sent the man tumbling out onto the porch. Rick shut the door and slid a nearby bookcase over to barricade it.

I turned back to Dom. He was still seated, staring down at Lyle who lay sprawled on his back in his pissy underpants, his remaining eye aimed up at the ceiling. Slowly, Dom shifted to face me. Our eyes met and held. Neither of us spoke.

Rick came back over and picked up the mason jar, drained the last of the moonshine. He glanced from Dom to me without comment, then picked up the dropped .38, went to the window and peeked out from behind the blinds.

Rick said, "There's a commotion over at the bunkhouse. Couple of guys just stepped outside, checking out that guy I shot."

"My boys are going to cut you down," Dom said. It was a simple statement of fact, with no heat to his words. In that moment he looked like a sad grampa, not a career criminal announcing my imminent death.

"You won't live to see it," I said.

"Didn't figure," Dom said. "You've known you were going to kill me before you ever heard what I had to say. This was never about revenge, you're just mad at the world 'cause you think you got dealt shitty cards. You can't kill the dealer, so you figure killing the player with the winning hand is the next best thing. Hell, you're probably mad I didn't give you more reason."

"You've given me plenty," I said. "You may not have killed Sally and Ernie yourself, but they're dead because of you just the same. Everything you are, everything you do, led us right here."

Dom looked back down at his dead son, said, "I could say the same to you."

I heard a car door slam, an engine starting.

Rick said, "Well, looks like the hookers are leaving. If nothing else, at least we stopped those boys from getting laid."

"Keep watching," I said.

"You mind if I light this?" Dom asked, waving his cigar toward the humidor. "Doctor made me give them up a few years ago. Bad for my heart he says. I just chew on 'em out of habit. Now seems like a good time to start up again."

"Go ahead," I said.

The pain in my chest had been a constant ache for the last several hours, but it grew worse now. My little Yobo was feeling neglected, needed to let me know she was still my one and only. I felt shaky, weak in the legs, like I needed to sit down. I tried to keep it together, keep my attention focused on Dom.

Dom lifted the lid to the humidor, reached inside. I raised my gun, waiting. Dom took out a lighter, held it up for me to see, then fired up the cigar, took several big puffs to get it going. He snapped the lighter shut and leaned his head back, blew a smoke ring.

Rick moved over and knelt by the bookcase blocking the door. "They're coming, Scotty. They're all outside now, looking this way. One guy's coming up on the porch."

A voice called from outside. "Dom? What's going on in there?"

I gave Dom a nod, keeping my gun pointed at his face.

Dom took a few more puffs from that cigar, said, "It okay, Tony. Everything's all right."

After a long pause, Tony said, "Lou's dead, Dom. He's out here. On the ground. Dead."

Dom said again, "It's okay. You boys just go back to your party."

Tony said, "The girls all left, Dom. There's no party tonight."

Rick looked over at me and gave a thumbs up.

Tony said, "I don't know if you heard me, but Lou's dead."

Dom said, "I heard you. Just go back to the bunkhouse, Tony."

Tony said, "This is weird, Dom. I'm coming inside."

Rick said, "The man told you to go the fuck away." He raised the .38 above the bookcase and fired blindly through the door.

I heard Tony yell out in surprise.

Rick took a quick look out the window. "They all went back inside the bunkhouse. I don't think they'll stay gone long, Scotty, so whatever the hell it is you plan to do you'd best do it."

Dom sat quietly puffing on his cigar. After a few seconds of that he said, "I forgot how satisfying this is. Never should have listened to that goddamn doctor."

Rick said, "Get ready. They're coming up the steps."

Dom returned the lighter to the humidor. I looked back at Rick, saw him turn away from the window.

"Watch it," he said.

I spun around, saw Dom pulling his hand back from the humidor holding a pistol. He fired and I heard Rick gasp behind me. I shot Dom in the chest and he sunk back into the chair, let the pistol drop to the floor.

Dom's eyes rolled around in his head, like he was having trouble focusing. Finally his gaze landed on me, then travelled down to the bullet hole in his chest. He let out a wheezy laugh around the cigar he still held clenched in his teeth.

Something about that laugh got to me. It was that feeling of being mocked. Like everything I'd gone through was merely an amusement for him. As his laugh grew stronger I stepped forward and I shot him a second time. Dom jerked, bit down in pain, and the broken cigar fell into his lap.

Dom's shine-soaked pants erupted into flames with a sudden 'whoof' sound. Next thing his shirt was ablaze, the fire licking up his body, then parting around his face like he was peering through a curtain of flame. Dom's eyes rolled around some more, and that laugh got louder and louder until it was almost a scream.

I looked away, saw Rick laying on the floor. He was on his back, both of his hands clutching at his throat, blood bubbling between his fingers.

Someone pounded on the cabin door. I heard a voice calling for Dom. Somebody else said they smelled something cooking. A third suggested getting something heavy to bust the door down.

Rick's lips were moving, but his voice was so soft I couldn't hear him. I knelt down, leaned in close, trying to make out his words.

In a gurgling whisper, Rick said, "Looks like I got my ending after all, Putt-Putt."

By now the curtains, books, even the wallpaper, were ablaze. Breathing grew difficult as the room filled with smoke. Rick's eyes shifted so that he was looking over my shoulder into the darkening haze. His hands fell from his throat, his face went slack, and in a voice more breath than sound, Rick said, "What was I so afraid of?"

All around the room flames licked up the walls and danced across the floor. Even though I could no longer see him, I could hear Dom's laugh rolling on and on, longer than seemed possible, until I had to consider that it was only in my head.

I heard a crash as the bookcase barring the door toppled over. I could see the shadowy figures of Dom's men entering the room. I shot at them and they shot back. I could hear them yelling, firing their guns, but louder than all of it was Dom's laugh.

A shadow moved near me and I fired, saw it go down, felt something hit me hard in the leg, the shoulder, and then a tearing pain as a third bullet hit me in the stomach.

Not to be outdone, my little Yobo finally took me into her embrace. A sharp, unbearable pain as she drove her dagger in deep. Then a flood of cold sensation, spreading out, filling me up.

I got to my feet despite how weak I felt. Or was that, like Dom's mad laughter, only in my mind? No matter. I had my ending as well.

I fired my last few rounds into the blinding smoke, and as the billowing darkness engulfed me, I took a final burning breath, and in a ragged voice cried out, "Suffering satellites, can this really be the-"

END

Liner Notes

I've always been fascinated by early television, particularly the kid's shows. The cheaper the production, the deeper my fondness. Despite having been made long before I was born, shows like Diver Dan, and Captain Video appeal to me more today than many of the shows I actually grew up watching. Part of the appeal is their value as historical artifacts. The other part comes from my viewing them as a triumph (or not) of creativity over an extremely limited budget. Having made a couple of low-budget movies myself, I always enjoy seeing folks create something from nothing.

I've wanted to tell a story about the cast and crew of a live kid's program for some time, and given my love for these shows, it would have been easy to romanticize their production. But the reality is, where I see them as a celebration of imagination and creativity, the folks who made them simply considered them a job. And not always one they enjoyed. With that in mind, I knew I wanted the story to be a bit dark, with at least a hint of reality seeping in around its pulpy edges.

The title came first. Just that title poking at my brain every once in a while, letting me know it was still there. Much like Scotty's little yobo, but without the fatal implications. And that was it for a good while, until one day I was reading about the DuMont Network (because I am a nerd) and discovered that they had actually purchased a UHF station right here in Kansas City.

DuMont was an early rival to the big three networks. Early on, in need of funding, they had sold an interest in the company to Paramount. Unfortunately for them, Paramount considered television to be a growing threat to the movie industry and did everything they could to interfere with the new medium's development in general, and DuMont in particular. Furthermore, DuMont's involvement with Paramount ultimately prevented them from getting the licenses necessary to acquire the stations they wanted, essentially blocking the network from reaching viewers. DuMont's purchase of KCTY was something of a Hail Mary pass, since few television owners at that time had UHF reception. But the network figured a small audience was better than no audience. Ultimately that audience was even smaller than expected, and by 1956 the DuMont network had ceased broadcasting altogether.

While those events do not seem rich with dramatic potential, knowing that DuMont had a direct connection to my hometown was exactly the spark I needed. After that the writing came fairly easily. It should be said that aside from DuMont's purchase of a local UHF station, everything else here is fictional.

-T.F.

About the Author

Timothy Friend is a Midwest based writer/filmmaker. He holds an MFA in Creative Writing and Media Arts from University of Missouri, Kansas City. He has written and directed two feature films, and his fiction has appeared in a variety of publications such as *Thuglit, Crossed Genres*, and N*eedle; a magazine of noir*.

New Crime. New Weird. New Pulp.

Visit us online at
www.coffinhop.com

Made in the USA
San Bernardino, CA
26 March 2018